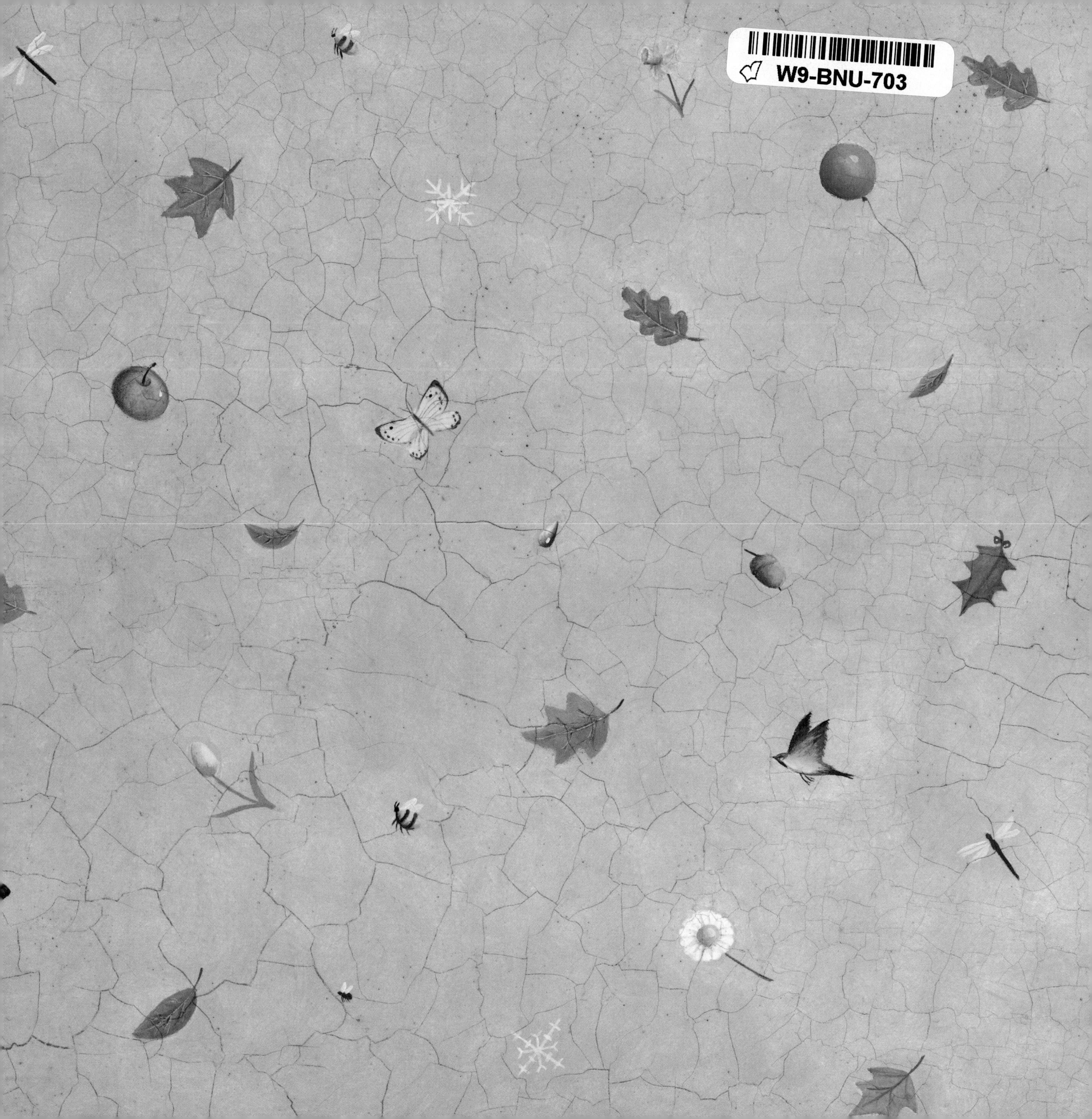

Listen, Listen

written by Phillis Gershator
illustrated by Alison Jay

Listen, listen . . . what's that sound? Insects singing all around!

Chirp, chirp, churr, churr, buzz, buzz, whirr, whirr.

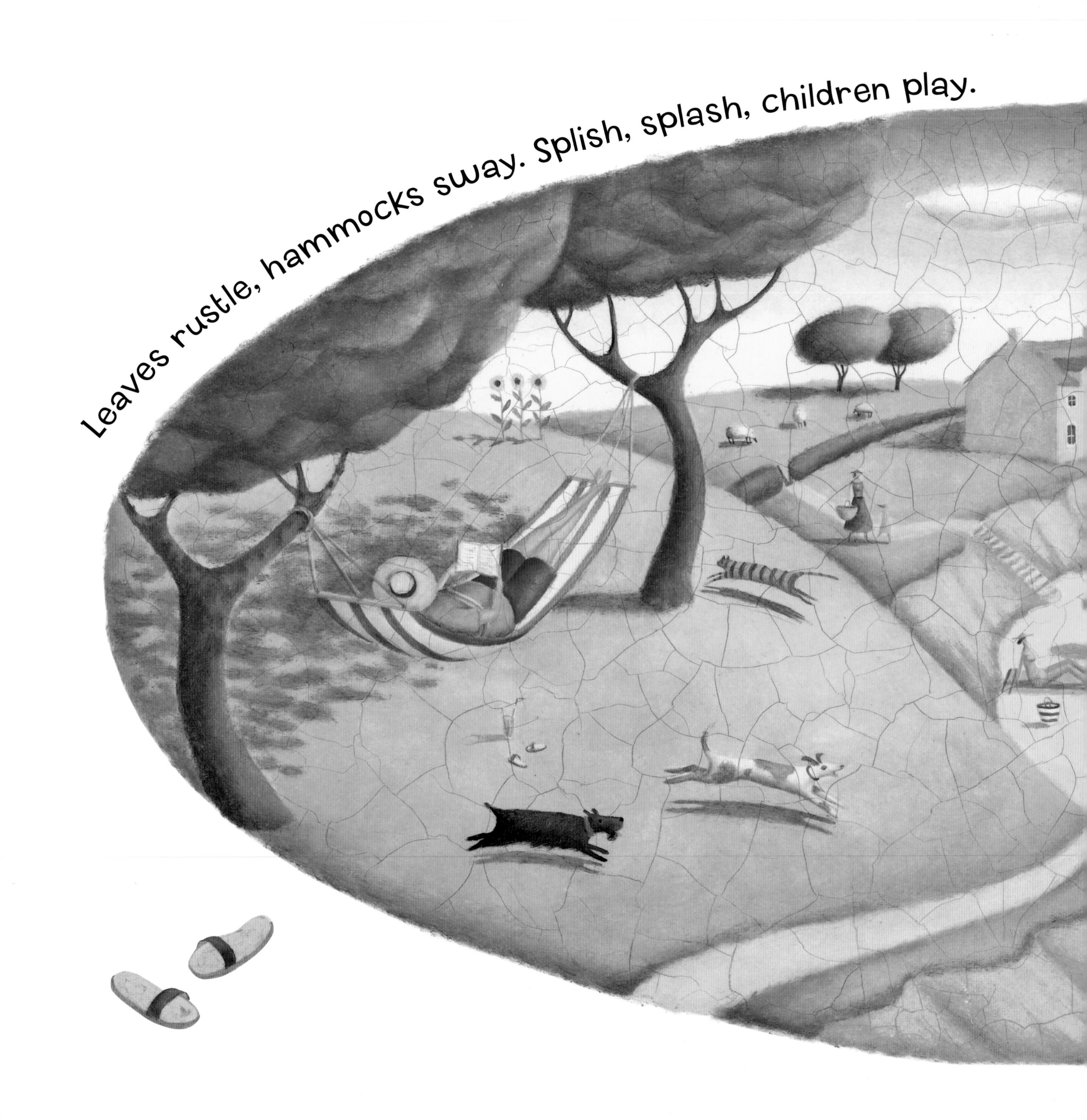

Leaves rustle, hammocks sway. Splish, splash, children play.

Clouds drift, dogs run. Sizzle, sizzle, summer sun.

Listen, listen . . . summer's gone. Good-bye insects, autumn's come.

Plop, plop, acorns drop. Hurry, scurry, squirrels hop.

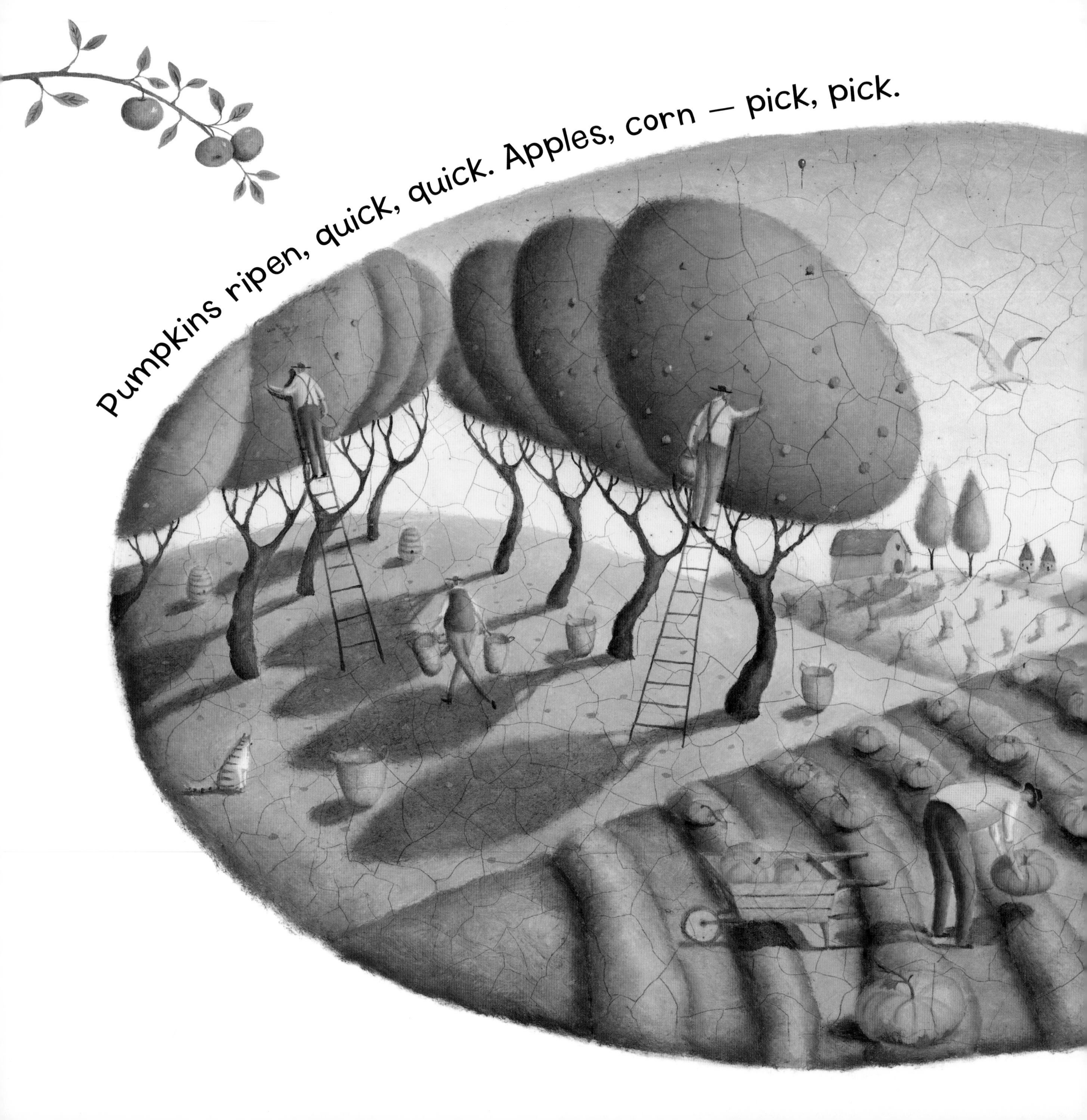

Pumpkins ripen, quick, quick. Apples, corn — pick, pick.

Crunch, crunch, people walk. Aak, aak, seagulls squawk.

Honk, honk, geese call. Swish, swish, leaves fall.

Whoosh, whoosh, hats fly. Whoo, whoo, owls cry.

Listen, listen . . . autumn's gone. Snowflakes whisper, "Winter's fun."

Shhh, shhh, snowy night. Snow sparkles, white, bright.

Crunch, crunch, boots clomp. Grown-ups shovel, children romp.

Skaters spin, skiers glide. Zip, zoom, slip, slide.

Brrr, brrr, warm-up time. Ooh, aah, candles shine.

Purr, purr, cats gaze. Crackle, crackle, fires blaze.

Listen, listen . . . winter's gone. Finches whistle, "Here's the sun!"

Pop, pop, bulbs sprout. Leaves grow, flowers shout.

Crick, crack, babies hatch. Peep, peep, chickens scratch.

Frogs croak, ducklings quack. Munch, munch, rabbits snack.

Rains fall, pitter, patter. Sparrows gather, chitter, chatter.

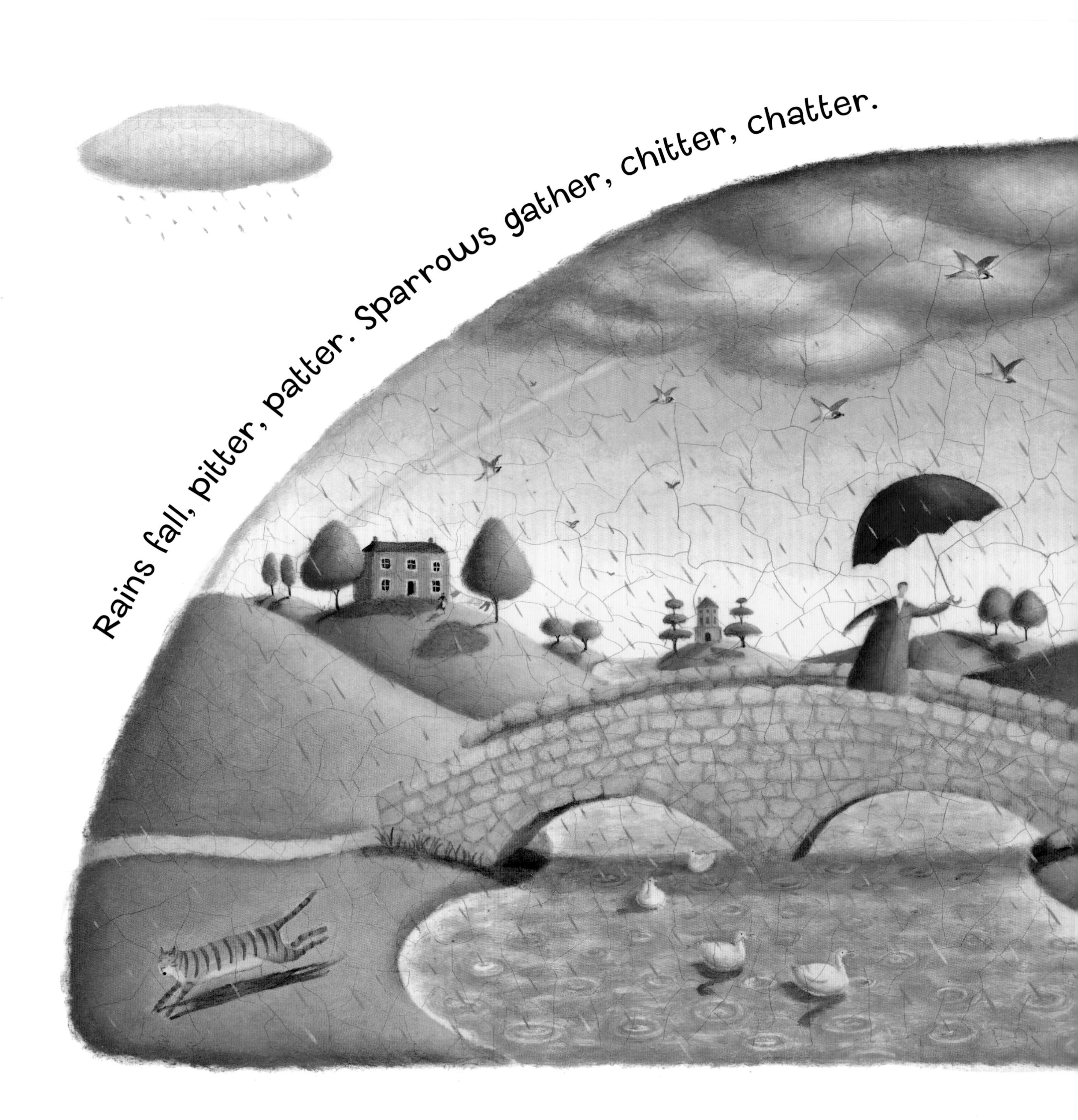

Listen, listen . . . spring is gone. Another season has begun.

In the air, on the ground, night and day — what's that sound?

Listen, listen . . . after spring, summer comes and . . .

Insects sing!

Chirp, chirp, churr, churr, buzz, buzz, whirr, whirr.

In the summer, can you see

a cricket

a butterfly

a mosquito

a bee

a dragonfly

a grasshopper

a beetle

a sunflower

a daisy

a leaf?

In the autumn, can you see

an owl

a goose

an acorn

a squirrel

a stalk of wheat

an apple

a pumpkin

an ear of corn

a seagull

a leaf?

In the winter, can you see

a crow

a starling

a snowflake

an icicle

a holly berry

a paw print

a mouse

a sprig of mistletoe

a leaf?

In the spring, can you see

a bluebell
a daffodil
a tulip
a sparrow
a chick
a rabbit
a duckling
a frog
a rainbow
a leaf?

To Tessa, for all seasons — P. G.
For Simon (S. P.), love from Alison (R. M.) xx — A. J.

Barefoot Books
124 Walcot Street
Bath, BA1 5BG, UK

Barefoot Books
2067 Massachusetts Ave
Cambridge, MA 02140, USA

First published in Great Britain by Barefoot Books, Ltd and in
the United States of America by Barefoot Books, Inc in 2007

This book has been printed on 100% acid-free paper
Reproduction by Grafiscan, Verona. Printed and bound in China by Printplus Ltd
Graphic design by Barefoot Books, Bath. This book was typeset in Present Black Condensed and Family Dog
The illustrations were prepared in alkyd oil paint on paper with a crackling varnish
Hardback ISBN 978-1-84686-084-3

British Cataloguing-in-Publication Data:
a catalogue record for this book is available from the British Library

1 3 5 7 9 8 6 4 2

Library of Congress Cataloging-in-Publication Data

Gershator, Phillis.
Listen, listen / Phillis Gershator ; Alison Jay.
p. cm.
Summary: Illustrations and rhyming text explore the sights and sounds
of nature in each season of the year.
ISBN-13: 978-1-84686-084-3 (alk. paper)
[1. Sound--Fiction. 2. Nature--Fiction. 3. Seasons--Fiction. 4. Stories
in rhyme.] I. Jay, Alison, ill. II. Title.
PZ8.3.G3235Lis 2008
[E]--dc22

2006100351

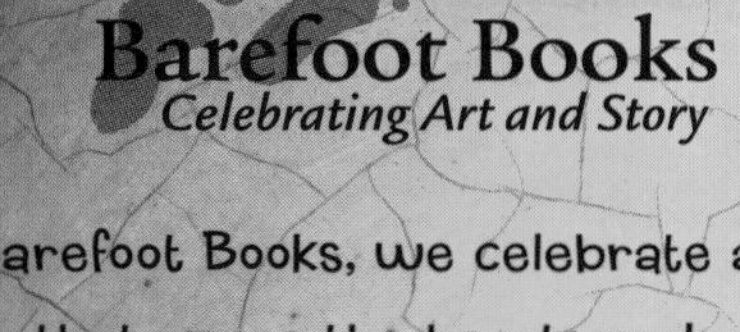

At Barefoot Books, we celebrate art and story that opens the hearts and minds of children from all walks of life, inspiring them to read deeper, search further, and explore their own creative gifts. Taking our inspiration from many different cultures, we focus on themes that encourage independence of spirit, enthusiasm for learning, and sharing of the world's diversity. Interactive, playful and beautiful, our products combine the best of the present with the best of the past to educate our children as the caretakers of tomorrow.

Live Barefoot!

Join us at www.barefootbooks.com

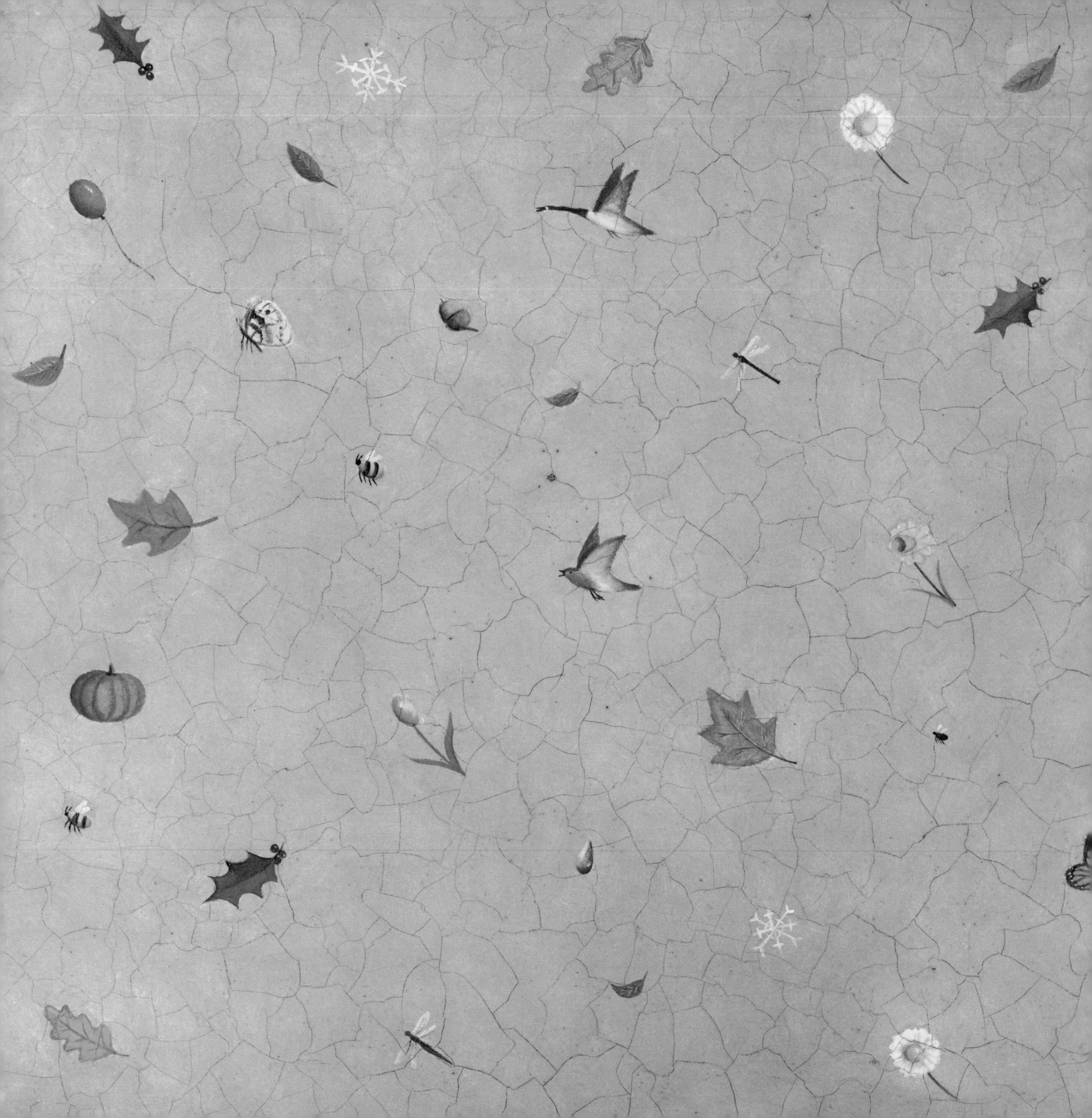